# Welcome to the world of Beast Quest!

Tom was once an ordinary village boy, until he travelled to the City, met King Hugo and discovered his destiny. Now he is the Master of the Beasts, sworn to defend Avantia and its people against Evil. Tom draws on the might of the magical Golden Armour, and is protected by powerful tokens granted to him by the Good Beasts of Avantia. Together with his loyal companion Elenna, Tom is always ready to visit new lands and tackle the enemies of the realm.

While there's blood in his veins, Tom will never give up the Quest…

There are special gold coins to collect in this book. You will earn one coin for every chapter you read.

Find out what to do with your coins at the end of the book.

# CONTENTS

*It is always said that Tangala has no Beasts. That, I'm pleased to say, is not quite true. There are Beasts here – terrifying ones – but they are sleeping. I will awaken them. I will fill them with rage and evil. And I will set them loose on the people of this kingdom.*

*Vakunda was my prison, but now I'm free. They thought I was dead. They were wrong.*

*I have lived for five hundred years. I have vanquished any who stood in my path. No puny Avantian boy will stop me now. My Beasts will ravage and destroy Tangala and I will stand over the ruins, ruler of all.*

*Zargon*

# 1

# A FALLEN HERO

Tom and Elenna skirted around a thorn bush then ducked under a hanging loop of vine. They were following their guide, Jed, through the forest. Tom ached all over. A gash on his arm, which he'd received falling from a flying chariot, itched and throbbed under its makeshift bandage. Elenna looked grey with exhaustion and her breathing sounded heavy in the muggy air.

Since they had begun their Quest to retrieve four powerful ancient weapons from the Evil Wizard Zargon, neither of them had slept. Zargon had stolen the weapons from the crypts beneath Queen Aroha's palace, and each was capable of waking an ancient Beast. Tom and Elenna had already defeated two such fearsome creatures – the last a giant, many-headed snake called Mallix. And, although he and Elenna were both battered and ready to drop with weariness, Tom knew they couldn't rest. Zargon would do everything in his power to unleash

the final two Beasts, and there was
no telling what havoc they would
wreak.

Jed, a tall young forest-dweller

with long red hair and engraved wooden armour, stopped and looked back, waiting for them to catch up. Jed didn't speak the common tongue, but he had become friends with Tom and Elenna since they saved his treetop village from Mallix's attack.

As Tom reached Jed's side, the boy lowered one hand palm downwards, signalling that they should rest. Tom sank gratefully on to a nearby tree stump and Elenna took a seat beside him.

"We can't be far from the edge of the forest now," Tom said.

Elenna nodded, then let out a sigh. Jed would soon return home to his village, but Tom and Elenna's journey was far from over. "If only we had some idea of where Zargon is headed," she said.

As Tom thought of the Evil Wizard's ability to transport himself at will, frustration welled inside him. "He could be anywhere in Tangala by now!"

"We have found him twice before. We'll find him again," Elenna said, but looking at her weary, grime-streaked face, Tom could see she wasn't convinced.

Suddenly, he heard a soft whickering sound through the trees. *A horse?*

Elenna turned her head, listening, while Jed's eyes widened in alarm.

"Do you think that could be Zargon?" Elenna whispered.

Beckoning for Jed to follow, Tom and Elenna set off in search of the horse. Their guide looked pale and anxious, freezing when the distant creature let out a snort.

*He's probably never seen a horse*, Tom realised. "Don't be afraid," he said, hoping to reassure the boy with his tone. Jed still looked uneasy, but he nodded and started off again.

Before long, the trees parted, revealing a small, grassy glade. Jed gasped at the sight of the chestnut mare standing at the centre. The horse was saddled and armoured, ready for battle. Her red-brown coat and black tail shone as if just brushed, and her silver armour glinted in the sun. A mossy white stone jutted from the grass at her feet. Tom could just make out some

writing carved into it as he slowly stepped towards the beautiful horse. "Hello...what are you doing here?" he murmured. The horse lifted her head, watching him from huge, gentle eyes. Tom reached for her bridle, but to his surprise, his hand went straight through the leather. The horse whinnied and shied away, her form suddenly shadowy and transparent. She broke into a canter and quickly disappeared into the trees.

*Some sort of vision?* Tom wondered. *A phantom?*

"*Na! Neala!*" Jed hissed. The boy was staring at the space where the horse had been.

"It's all right," Tom said, but Jed

shook his head fiercely, then turned and sprinted away into the forest.

Elenna frowned and pointed to the white stone. "It looks like a grave marker," she said.

Tom bent and scraped away the moss that covered the writing. "'Here lies Roger'," he read aloud. "He must be buried here. I wonder who he was..."

"*I* am Roger," said a low, hollow voice. Tom turned to see a tall, armoured man step from the treeline. Pulse racing, Tom reached for the hilt of his sword. The stranger seemed maybe twenty years of age, with a sparse, neatly trimmed dark beard and grey eyes. As Roger turned and

let out a whistle, Tom noticed with a sudden chill that he could see right through the warrior's frame. The soft thud of hooves answered Roger's whistle, and a moment later, the armoured mare trotted to his side. Roger smiled and stroked her glossy mane as she nuzzled his shoulder. "This is Windspur," Roger told Tom and Elenna. "She's rather nervous of strangers. Although, from your shield, I think you must be a Master of the Beasts?"

"I am," Tom said, bowing his head. "And one of my powers is being able to communicate with previous Masters. You must be one of the fallen warriors whose weapons the Evil Wizard Zargon stole. I have already met Celesta, the Mistress of the Beasts who defeated Teknos. I am honoured to meet another of Tangala's heroes."

Roger looked down bashfully. "I'm not sure I really count as a hero," he said. "I perished on my very first Quest. And I was never awarded the title of Master of the Beasts in life – only after I fell defeating Mallix."

"Those who lay down their lives defending the innocent are the truest heroes of all," Elenna told the young man. "Mallix was a fearsome foe – it took both of us together to defeat him. But our Quest isn't over. Zargon is planning to raise two more Beasts, unless we find them first."

"Well, I can help you with that, at least," Roger said, flashing them a rueful smile. "Silexa the Stone Cat stirs in the lost City of Viga, roughly two days' ride from here."

Tom's heart sank. "Without horses, we'll never get there in time to stop Zargon!"

Roger smiled again, more broadly this time, and patted the mare's flank. "Windspur will take you. She was the fastest steed in all of Tangala when she lived. Now, she is faster still. She will have you in Viga before noon." His expression turned suddenly anxious again. "But you will need to leave at once if you are to prevent disaster there. If Silexa wakes, many innocent people will perish."

Tom nodded. "We will go now." He put out a hand to beckon Windspur.

The mare gave a friendly snort and clopped towards him. To Tom's relief, her red-brown coat and dark mane looked solid and glossy once more. He let her nuzzle his hand with her soft nose, which felt reassuringly warm – she even smelled of sweet hay and stables, just like a living horse. Tom swallowed his remaining unease and leapt into the saddle. After a moment's hesitation, Elenna swung up behind him.

"I wish you good speed!" Roger said, his voice fading to a distant echo. Tom turned to wave goodbye, but found only the lone white stone, standing in the centre of the sunny glade. Roger had vanished. Tom felt a pang of sorrow for the young warrior, buried far from home. But suddenly Windspur tossed her head and set off, so fast his thoughts were scattered. With a yelp of surprise, Elenna grabbed Tom's waist and they both clung on for their lives as the phantom horse sped away through the forest.

# THE LOST CITY

Tom craned low over Windspur's neck while Elenna clung tightly to his waist. On either side of them, trees swept by in streaks of green and brown. The horse's movement was fluid and smooth, but the speed of the ride snatched Tom's breath away – it was like being drawn along on a swift current. Tom tugged on the

reins, hoping to slow the mare, but Windspur let out a joyful neigh and cantered on faster than ever. Soon the landscape sped by so quickly, Tom saw nothing but flashes of colour and streaks of light and dark. He clamped his legs tightly about the horse's sides and let the wild rush of wind and colour buffet past him. The smooth motion was strangely lulling, and his mind began to drift...
*How long have we been riding?*
He couldn't be sure. Time itself seemed to have blurred, just like the landscape...

And then all at once, without a jolt or any sign of slowing down, they were still.

The sudden quiet made Tom's ears ring. He shook his head. Elenna slowly unclamped her arms from around his waist, and they both looked around. They were on the outskirts of what must once have been a beautiful city. But now, only broken columns and shattered buildings, made from huge sandstone blocks, rose from the desert. Tom got unsteadily down from the saddle, his muscles stiff from clinging on. Elenna quickly joined him.

"Thank you for carrying us so swiftly!" Tom told Windspur. But when he reached out to pat the horse's flank, his hand found only empty air. She had vanished, without leaving so much as a hoof-print behind.

Tom turned back to the ruined city before them. Drifts of sand had built up against those few walls that remained standing. The silence was broken only by the mournful wail of the wind blowing through cracked brickwork.

"This place is eerie," Elenna murmured. "Roger said there were people in danger. But whoever lived here must have left long ago."

Tom nodded. "It almost looks like there was an earthquake."

"Or several," Elenna agreed, looking around at the devastation. "We'd better explore."

They started off through the remains of a high arch, and down a sandy street lined with fallen columns. Many of the buildings had been reduced to just their foundations, but others had dark windows that looked like watchful eyes. As they walked, Tom noticed shards of broken pottery lying about, still showing traces of bright paint. They passed horse troughs, worn shallow and smooth by the wind and time, and even a carved stone mouse that looked like some kind of child's toy. Tom found himself thinking of the people that must have dwelt here long ago. *I hope they made it out alive when the end came.*

Soon, they reached a deserted
plaza surrounded by buildings – all
damaged beyond repair, but with
archways and carvings that showed
that they had once been grand and
beautiful. A dusty mosaic, badly

cracked and missing pieces, filled the
centre of the square. Tom and Elenna
stepped in for a closer look.

"A giant cat!" Elenna exclaimed,
pointing to the depiction of a slender
black creature sitting on its haunches,

with haughty, emerald eyes. "Roger said Silexa was a cat – but it looks as if the people here worshipped her."

"Yes…" Tom frowned as he squinted down at the smaller sculptures at the base of the statue, of strange folk kneeling before Silexa. They all had triangular ears on the tops of their heads, and what appeared to be whiskers. "And look, they're wearing cat-masks!"

A high, yowling screech cut the air, making Tom's heart hammer. It had come from up ahead. He drew his sword. "Someone's in trouble!"

They both leapt into a run, pounding through the deserted

streets, searching for any sign of life. Another cry, nearer this time, sent Tom racing down a side alley into another open square surrounded by high, carved pillars. Tom gasped – a boy hovered in the air at the centre of the space, his legs kicking and his hands clawing at his throat as if something were strangling him. The child gave a hideous, choking scream. Tom started forwards, but Elenna caught his arm.

"Zargon!" she hissed, pointing towards a pillar about a dozen paces away.

Tom saw the edge of a black cloak, and a muscular forearm reaching from behind the column,

fingers curled in the air as if gripping
something invisible. *He's using magic
to strangle the boy!*

Tom signalled for Elenna to go one
way around the pillar, then silently
ran the other way. But as he skirted

behind the wizard, his boot struck a loose stone and sent it skittering. He cursed under his breath as Zargon turned.

With a theatrical sigh, the wizard rolled his eyes.

"You again?" he said, then tightened his curled fingers in the air, making the struggling boy gasp with pain.

"Stop!" Tom cried, lifting his sword as Elenna aimed an arrow at the wizard's chest.

"You two are harder to kill than cockroaches," Zargon drawled. Then his eyes narrowed, and he bared his teeth. "I won't fail again."

# ATTACK!

"Let the child go!" Tom demanded, holding Zargon's cruel gaze.

"With pleasure," the wizard answered, smiling coldly. As he lowered his hand, the boy let out a terrified yelp and plummeted towards the ground. Horror gripped Tom. *He'll be killed!* But the child somehow twisted in the air, landing lightly on all fours.

"Leave now, or I'll put an arrow through that magic hand of yours!" Elenna growled.

"Oh, but I'm just starting to enjoy myself," Zargon said. On the ground, the boy looked dazed and pale. He shook himself, but oddly, stayed on his hands and feet.

"I warned you!" Elenna snapped, and let her arrow fly. With the speed of a striking snake, Zargon snatched the arrow from the air, and snapped it in two.

"Pathetic!" he said, letting the broken missile fall. "I've got more important things to do than play your childish games." His lips twisted with

spite and he shot a blast of purple
energy towards a listing column of
stone, right beside the fallen child.
The boy looked up, eyes widening in
fear, then turned and fled, moving
fast on his hands and feet...but

not fast enough. With a sickening crash, the pillar hit the ground and shattered, burying the child in rubble.

With a roar of fury, Tom lunged for the wizard, his sword drawn back to strike. Zargon lifted his other hand, and Tom noticed a heavy-looking mace swinging towards him just before it slammed into his ribs, throwing him sideways, into a wall. He slid to the ground, gasping with agony. Swallowing the sickness rising in his throat, he staggered up and looked for the wizard. A hollow cackle echoed through the plaza. Zargon had vanished.

"Help me!" Elenna called, shifting the rubble that covered the boy.

Wincing in pain with each movement, Tom joined her in heaving the larger pieces away, soon uncovering the child's form – curled tightly in a ball.

"He's breathing!" Elenna cried, turning the boy over. His face was dusty, with a bloody gash across the forehead, but his chest rose and fell evenly, and his limbs looked straight and uninjured – although oddly sinewy and long. Tom suddenly noticed how unusual his features were. He had wide-set eyes, thin lips and a flat nose, along with what looked like silvery whiskers sprouting from his cheeks – like a cat's. And the boy's ears, which had been flicked back and hidden by his sandy hair,

now stuck up in two points. *How strange! That's no mask...*

Tom hurriedly took Epos's healing talon from its place in his shield, remembering with a pang of worry that his shield had been struck by lightning during their recent chariot ride, and how the magic tokens had failed him since. Though he had scrubbed the wood clean of soot with fresh grass, making the tokens shine like new, he hadn't tested their powers. He hoped with all his heart that time had restored them.

Gently touching the talon against the boy's bleeding head, he held his breath, willing it to work. *Yes!* The edges of the cut knitted together, leaving only a smudge of blood. Elenna gently shook the boy's shoulder.

The child's eyes snapped open – emerald green, with narrow, slitted pupils. They widened in alarm as they rested on Tom and Elenna, and in a sudden scrabble of movement, the boy flipped over on to all fours and let out a hiss. His teeth were pointed, and the nails on his hands and bare feet curved to wicked points too.

"We won't harm you!" Elenna said, rearing away as the boy arched his back and hissed again, swiping with his sharp claws. "We're trying to help!"

But the boy turned and sped away, pouncing over the rubble. Tom noticed a green pendant tied to a broken leather thong lying among the debris and picked it up.

"You dropped this!" he called,
but the boy had already vanished
between two half-ruined buildings.

"So, the city isn't deserted after
all," Elenna said.

Tom nodded. "I wonder if there are
other people like him here?"

Elenna frowned thoughtfully.
"Tangala has many tribes, but I've
never heard of a race of cat-folk.
Maybe they have lived here since the
city was whole. I wonder why they
didn't find somewhere new? It can't
be easy surviving among these ruins."

"All the more reason to make
sure Zargon doesn't cause more
damage!" Tom said. He started off
again with Elenna at his side. They

both trod softly, looking all about as they went, listening for any slight movement from the strange residents of the city, or from a Beast.

The back of Tom's neck prickled uncomfortably in the silence, and though the sun beat down, the hairs on his arms stood on end. As he picked his way through the rubble, shadowy movements flickered at the edges of his vision, but each time he turned, there was nothing to see.

"We're being watched," he whispered to Elenna.

She nodded, then her eyes widened, and she pointed. Tom looked and saw that a line of figures had appeared on top of a wall ahead of them –

rangy men and women, dressed in tunics, but crouched like cats, ready to pounce. Tom saw that all had the same pointed ears and bright, widely spaced eyes as the boy.

Tom swallowed as more cat-people prowled from dark doorways and slunk from shadowy nooks, flexing their sharp claws and baring their fangs. Their tunics were worn and tattered, but with brightly jewelled belts clasped about the waist. Many wore bangles and necklaces, too. But Tom couldn't see any weapons. *Except for their claws and teeth*, he thought, keeping his hand on the hilt of his sword.

"We come as friends," Tom called,

hoping the people would understand.
"We mean no harm."

"Then why are you here?" a young
woman demanded, leaping down
to stand upright at the base of the
wall. She had a fluffy halo of white
hair and blazing blue-green eyes.
Although she spoke the common
tongue, her words were slow and
stretched out. "Why do you trespass
in our sacred city?"

"We are here to defeat an Evil
Wizard," Tom said. He lifted his
hands, showing he had no intention
of drawing his sword.

The woman hissed. "Where did you
find that?" she asked, pointing to
the green pendant that still dangled

from Tom's fingers.

"A young boy was wearing it," Tom answered. "He was hurt by the wizard we seek. We tried to help him, but he ran away. We are here to find Silexa – can you help us?"

A terrific yowl of rage greeted his words as every one of the cat-folk lunged toward them at once, claws flying and teeth bared.

Tom threw up his shield. Elenna brandished her bow like a fighting staff. Tom could barely make out one attacker from the next, they crowded so close. Each time he shoved someone back with his shield, another furious man or woman took their place. Claws raked at

his skin and clothes, ripping and tearing. Screams of rage filled his ears. More cat-people joined the fight. Tom backed away, but stumbled on a loose piece of rock and fell. Through the mass of bodies, he saw Elenna trip too. He scrambled into a crouch and managed to lift his shield, but a muscular man with black hair and a torn ear pounced at him, knocking it from his hands and shoving him over. Tom kicked the man away, then shielded his face with his arms, bracing himself as a new wave of attackers surged forwards. Day seemed to turn to night, as all light was blocked by the mass of clawed, hissing cat-folk bundling on top of him.

# SILEXA'S TEMPLE

A high-pitched screech broke
through the hisses and yowls.
The slashing, clawing mob that
surrounded Tom fell back. He
scrambled up, breathing hard and
covered in bleeding scratches, to see
the young boy he and Elenna had
rescued crouched high on a wall. The
child let out another urgent meow.

Elenna had curled into a ball, but now rose, her eyes wild and her skin crisscrossed with cuts. She let out a shaking breath.

The crowd of cat-folk had all turned towards the small boy, watching as he leapt from the wall and scampered towards the white-haired woman on all fours. Then he stood upright and started speaking in a series of yowls, waving his arms, occasionally pointing at Tom and Elenna. *I hope he's on our side!* Tom thought. The white-haired woman glanced their way, eyes narrowed suspiciously. But the rest of the cat-folk seemed calmer, their ears pricked as they listened to the child, and their bristling hair settling to lie flat. Tom pushed himself up to standing. The boy glanced his way again and smiled tentatively.

Tom returned the smile. "Here, take this!" he called, throwing the boy the emerald pendant. The lad caught it, and quickly tied it around his neck. After regarding them coolly for a moment with sea-green eyes, the white-haired young woman stalked towards Tom and Elenna. Tom bowed his head respectfully, glad to notice that her claws were sheathed, and her fangs covered, though her lips were pressed together in a tight, grim line.

"My name is Aleesa," the cat-

woman said, glancing at each of them in turn. "My boy, Ezra, tells me you saved his life, and that you have good hearts. But who is the other man you spoke of? He tried to kill Ezra. Why?

We are a quiet people, defenceless, and without enemies."

His whole body smarting with cuts, Tom wasn't so sure about the 'defenceless' part, but he let it go. "The man is called Zargon. He is an Evil Wizard, who plans to awaken Silexa."

Aleesa's hair bristled, and her eyes flashed with anger. "He will not disturb our spirit guide. Silexa resides at the heart of our city, and has been hidden for centuries. No one but us knows where she rests."

Ezra mewed, and sheepishly lifted a clawed hand. His mother turned to him. Without meeting her gaze, Ezra meowed a few words, his ears and whiskers drooping.

When he'd finished, Aleesa closed her eyes for a moment, her pointed teeth clenched. Rumbling growls and muttered meows ran through the gathered people as they exchanged uneasy glances. Aleesa turned back to Tom and Elenna.

"Ezra says that in his fear, he told the wizard where to find our guide. We have all pledged to protect her peace, and to ensure no outsider ever finds her. If what you say is true, and Zargon knows how to awaken her spirit, he must be stopped."

"Then lead us to her," Tom said. "We have stopped Zargon twice before. We will do so again."

Aleesa held Tom's gaze for a long

moment, her blue-green eyes full of indecision. Then she let out a sigh.

"This goes against everything we stand for. But this wizard must not be allowed to disturb Silexa. If you help us, we will lead you to her now."

"While there's blood in my veins, I will do everything in my power to stop Zargon," Tom said.

Aleesa nodded once, then stalked away, glancing back briefly to make sure Tom and Elenna were following. The rest of the cat-people joined them too, pacing almost silently on all fours, some flanking Tom and Elenna, padding over the rubble-strewn ground, while others kept to the broken walls, agile and light-footed.

As Tom and Elenna caught up
with Aleesa, she gestured around
herself with one clawed hand.
"Many thousands used to dwell in
our city," she said. "I am told that it
was beautiful, and filled with music
and laughter. But then a terrible
earthquake hit. Most of the people
fled. Only the priests and priestesses
who devoted their lives to Silexa
remained. We are their distant
descendants, and we carry on their
work."

As the group travelled deeper
into the city, Tom noticed that the
buildings looked less damaged.
They passed carved water fountains
and elegant statues, some almost

intact. While the outskirts of the
city were barren and dry, here vines
and creepers trailed along the dusty
ground and grew up the ancient
brickwork.

Finally, Aleesa led them along
a wide road lined with massive
columns, towards a huge square
temple with a pointed roof. Six
colossal pillars, twined round with
vegetation, spanned the front of the
building; and beyond them, Tom
could see an entrance, partly blocked
with rubble. Aleesa climbed a wide
flight of steps that led up to the
shadowy entrance, then stopped. Tom
peered into inky silence as still as a
tomb – there was no sign of Zargon.

*Maybe we've made it in time!*

"We will need to go inside," he told Aleesa. She nodded curtly. Tom drew his sword, and Elenna lifted her bow. They both exchanged a wary glance, then stepped into the building. Cool shade greeted them, along with the smell of dust and crumbling stone. Shafts of sunlight glanced through chinks in the ceiling, dimly illuminating a colonnade leading towards a carved, square plinth the size of a cart. Aleesa let out a gasp of dismay as her eyes fell on the empty pedestal.

"Silexa is gone!" she hissed. Yowls of horror went up from behind Tom as more of the cat-people filed into

the gloom. In the darkness at the back
of the chamber, something stirred.
Tom drew back his sword as an all-
too-familiar figure stepped from
behind the mighty plinth. *Zargon!*
The wizard smiled broadly, his eyes

shining and triumphant. He lifted
the mace he had stolen from the
palace crypt and gestured to the
empty pedestal.

"As you can see, you are too late,"
he said. "Silexa has awoken, and all
shall perish in her wrath!"

# 5

# SILEXA STRIKES

Tom watched, dread twisting in his gut as the deep shadows beyond the wizard darkened and coalesced into a solid shape, broad and impossibly tall — a colossal cat with six red eyes. With a chorus of sharp hisses, the cat-people sank to their knees, heads bent in worship.

"No!" Tom told them. "This is not

the Silexa you know. This Beast has been enchanted by Evil." The giant cat, broad-shouldered and powerfully muscled, bared her fangs and let out a long, low growl. Though her inky fur looked velvety soft, her teeth

gleamed like volcanic glass and curved inwards, as deadly as scythes. Her huge eyes blazed with fury. Tom brandished his blade and shield and hunkered down, ready to fight. Behind him, Elenna aimed an arrow

towards the Beast.

"Kill them all!" Zargon cried, gesturing at the gathered cat-folk with his mace.

With the blood-curdling scream of a striking panther, Silexa leapt over the plinth. The cat-folk scattered as the Beast landed, growling and snapping. Elenna fired, striking the creature's chest, but her arrow shattered on impact.

More cries filled the air. Most of the cat-folk were racing for the entrance, but one smoky-haired woman crouched, frozen in place, watching Silexa with wide amber eyes. Snarling fiercely, the Beast swiped a paw at the woman. Tom threw himself in the way, shield raised. *BOOF!* The power of the strike slammed him to his knees.

"Run!" Elenna screamed.

"Everyone, get out of here!"

Staggering up, Tom saw Zargon slip from the chamber, almost hidden by the surge of cat-folk scrambling for the exit. Elenna fired another arrow at Silexa, then another — but each one splintered to shards without leaving a mark. Silexa narrowed her glowing eyes and turned on Elenna, hissing with rage. Elenna took aim and fired straight for Silexa's throat, but the Beast was too fast and dodged her arrow.

"Go after Zargon!" Tom cried. "Your arrows aren't working, and we can't let him escape. I'll fight Silexa." Elenna glanced towards the door behind her, then back at Silexa, who was poised and ready to leap.

"I'll be back!" she told Tom, then sprinted after the wizard.

"I'm over here!" Tom called to the Beast. Silexa swung around, and swiped a massive paw at Tom's throat. Tom leapt sideways, the Beast's claws just catching his arm. Drawing a sharp intake of breath at the sudden pain, he backed further into the shadows. Silexa prowled after him, head low and red eyes glowing with the hungry light of a hunter stalking its prey. Tom surveyed the giant cat, looking for any sign of a weakness. But all he could see were her bulging muscles, curved talons, and sharp black teeth as long as his arm. He took another step backwards, then another. His heels struck the wall behind him. *I'm cornered!* Silexa's red eyes flashed with triumph. She crouched, tail twitching, and coiled her muscles, ready to pounce.

Tom lifted his sword and shield, but he knew they'd be no match for Silexa's deadly claws. *Or her speed. Unless I can outwit her...*

Something clicked into place in Tom's mind.

"Come on, then!" he called, using the power of the red jewel in his belt to communicate with the Beast. Silexa let out a harsh, wild, killing cry, and leapt. At the same moment, Tom called on the power of his golden armour, ducked his head and ran. The Beast gave a furious snarl as she soared over Tom. He raced on, only stopping when he reached the far side of the chamber. He spun just as Silexa thudded headfirst into the wall where he'd been standing. *CRASH!* The ancient brickwork exploded outwards, flooding the room with light. Huge chunks of stone smashed down from the ceiling, tumbling off Silexa's fur, coating her with dust. She shook her head, then turned, her red eyes flaming bright, and burning with pure hatred and fury.

Tom lifted his sword and waved it. "I'm still here!" he called tauntingly. "You'll have to be much quicker than that!" All around him, bricks were falling, cracks tracing their way up the walls, and across what remained of the ceiling. He glanced back to see the doorway behind him crumbling, filling with stone. A chunk of masonry hit his shoulder, sending a bolt of pain down his shield-arm. *I have to get out! Now!*

"What are you waiting for?" Tom shouted. Growling deep in her throat, Silexa bunched her muscles and leapt, deadly claws outstretched and jaws wide open. Tom held his ground for an instant longer, then turned. A slab of rock plummeted towards him. He dodged right, then powered on, sprinting for the exit, which was now nearly blocked with rubble. With a final, desperate burst of speed, he reached the opening, angled his body sideways and pushed through. Jagged edges of stone tore at his back as he burst out into daylight, stumbling a few more paces, and almost overbalancing as he clambered down the stairs.

*SMASH!* Choking dust filled his lungs. The roar of falling masonry echoed behind him. A wail of anguish went up from the gathered cat-folk ahead.

"Run!" Tom cried. The people scattered. Tom ran with them, racing through the colonnade away from the deadly barrage of rubble. He turned just in time to see the temple's stone pillars lean, then

topple, shattering and sending chunks of sandstone tumbling over the ground. Beyond the fallen pillars, a huge pile of broken masonry and a cloud of billowing dust were all that remained of the temple. Silexa was buried somewhere beneath.

# 6

# BEAST OF SMOKE
# AND STONE

*She's defeated!* Tom thought,
doubled over with exhaustion and
pain.

The cat-people crowded close
together, filling the space between
the pillars of the colonnade, some
kneeling with their heads bowed,
others weeping openly. Small

stones still shifted in the rubble. Tom looked for Elenna and quickly found her near the back of the group. She had an arrow trained at point-blank range on Zargon's chest. Aleesa stood at her side, sharp teeth bared and claws raised. Her cheeks were wet with tears, but her blue-green eyes blazed as she glared at the wizard, who scowled back at his captors. Tom stormed towards him through the throng of distraught cat-people.

"It's over!" Tom cried as he reached Zargon. "You will return with us to the palace to face Queen Aroha's justice!"

The wizard's eyes flashed with

anger and he started to lift a hand.

Elenna's bow creaked. "I told you, one move, and I loose this arrow!" she snapped. Zargon took a step back and let his hand fall.

All around them, the cat-folk howled in anguish. Tom could hear the name 'Silexa' repeated over and over, along with other words he didn't understand. But he knew their meaning. Pain and grief – all because of Zargon. He glanced back at the ruined temple, a terrible sorrow rising inside him. *Silexa was a Good Beast, driven to destroy by Zargon's Evil. She didn't deserve to die like that!*

"I would kill you now," Aleesa told the wizard, her voice hoarse with emotion, "but that would end your suffering. I hope you rot in darkness for all eternity!"

"While there is blood in my veins, Zargon will pay dearly for his

crimes," Tom promised Aleesa.
Suddenly, he felt a pulse of warmth
from the red jewel in his belt. A
rasping hiss filled his mind — little
more than a soft whisper, but dark
with menace...

*You cannot kill me so easily, little*
*mouse. I am coming for my prey and*
*this time, none shall escape my teeth.*

"Silexa lives!" Tom gasped. He
glanced again towards the ruined
temple, seeing dark tendrils of
smoke snaking up from between
the bricks. "Look!" He turned to
point. The smoke thickened and
swirled, drawing together into an
impenetrable black cloud. Six red
eyes appeared in the darkness before

the cloud solidified, taking the form of a giant black cat which stood on all fours upon the ruins of the temple, her tail twitching and her fur bristling. The cat-people fell silent. Those still standing dropped to their knees, arms outstretched in reverence.

"Tell your people to flee," Tom told Aleesa. "I will release Silexa from Zargon's Evil – but you must hide."

From her vantage point on top of the ruined temple, Silexa lifted her head and let out a wild roar, then gathered herself on her haunches, poised to attack.

"Go, now!" Tom cried.

There was a fizzing sound, and
Elenna yelped. Tom turned to see
her tumble to the ground, clutching
her chest. Zargon's hands, raised
before him, crackled with energy
and his lips were drawn back in a
rictus of hate. Before Tom could do
anything, the wizard sent another
sizzling bolt of energy towards
Aleesa, throwing her backwards
through the air. At the same
moment, Silexa bounded down
from the pile of ruins. The cat-folk
scattered as she landed among
them, diving out of range of her
lashing claws. Wide-eyed with panic
and confusion, men and women
leapt for shelter behind columns

and darted into crumbling buildings.

With her other prey gone, Silexa turned and fixed her glowing eyes on Tom. He drew back his sword as she prowled towards him, her ears flicked back, her head lowered, and her huge teeth opened in a snarl. Zargon turned and ran.

Tom was torn. Part of him wanted to chase the wizard, but he knew his first duty was to save the cat-folk from the Beast. He stood his ground, watching as the vast creature stalked closer. He kept his shield raised, and his weight down on the balls of his feet. Silexa padded silently onwards, a low growl rumbling in her throat. Tom did not move, but kept his eyes locked on the Beast's, waiting for her to come within reach. Up close, he could see the deadly glint of her fangs, and the crazed hunger blazing in her six red eyes. *Now!* Tom stabbed at Silexa's chest. As his sword found its mark, Silexa's body dissolved, vanishing in a swirling cloud of smoke. Already committed, Tom staggered and almost fell. He managed to catch his balance, and lifted his blade once more, but there was nothing to strike. He clenched his teeth. *How can I fight a Beast made of smoke and stone?*

"Tom, look out!" Elenna cried. He spun to see Silexa crouched right behind him, solid once more – vast

and muscled. With deadly speed, she
lunged, snapping for his face. Tom
blocked with his shield, feeling the
immense impact as the cat's curved
fangs sank into the wood.

Yowling with anger, Silexa shook her head, wrenching Tom off his feet and jolting him from side to side like a ragdoll. He somehow kept his grip on his shield, his joints straining. Silexa jerked her neck sideways, letting the shield go and sending Tom flying through the air. He landed in a heap, cracking his elbow so hard against the ground he felt the bone shatter with a sickening pain. Black spots filled his vision. He tried to scramble up, but bile rose in his throat and he sank back to the ground.

Elenna raced to his side, hand outstretched to help him up. Beyond her, Tom could see Silexa, crouched back on her haunches, her huge muscles flexing, ready to attack once more. Elenna grabbed Tom's good wrist and pulled him to his feet. He half-staggered, half-ran, dizzy and sick with pain as she yanked him towards the nearest building and through a narrow opening that was almost blocked with stone.

Inside, the space was dim, with the only light coming through cracks in the walls. Tom sank to the ground, wanting nothing more than to close his eyes, to sleep – anything to block out the agony.

"We don't have long," Elenna told him. "Silexa will smash this place to pieces. We need a plan."

Tom swallowed his sickness and tried to focus, but he could hardly think through the agony in his elbow.

"Epos's talon!" Elenna said urgently.

*Of course!* Tom thought. *At least I managed to keep hold of my shield!* He snatched the flame bird's healing talon from its place and held it against his injured arm. As the pain receded, his mind cleared, and his senses sharpened. He could hear Silexa pacing outside. But as he listened, the sounds stopped abruptly. Tom and Elenna looked at each other, holding their breath. Somehow, the ominous silence felt even more threatening than Silexa's rumbling growl.

Tom crossed to a jagged crack in
the wall and peered through. The
ruins outside were deserted, with no
sign of the Beast. He felt a glimmer
of relief that the cat-folk were safe.

"Tom!" Elenna hissed, grabbing
his arm. He turned to see tendrils
of black smoke seeping through the
walls — shadowy at first, but quickly
thickening and drawing together
into an inky clot of darkness. Then
six red eyes appeared, burning with
hatred.

# AN INVISIBLE FOE

"Get out!" Tom shouted to Elenna. They both dived for the narrow exit and scrambled through, out into daylight, just as a terrific crash erupted behind them. Chunks of stone pounded against Tom's back and shoulders as he raced onwards. Finally, he turned to see the building gone, and in its place,

Silexa standing tall among the scattered ruins. Her dark coat was covered in brick dust and chips of stone, but as Tom and Elenna watched, she shook herself clean, then fixed them with her furious gaze.

"Split up!" Tom cried. He and Elenna sprinted over uneven ground littered with broken masonry. Elenna veered right, and Tom ducked left, heading for the colonnade. Glancing back, he saw Silexa briefly look at Elenna before focusing her blazing hunter's gaze on him. He raced on, soon reaching the first stone column. Calling on the magic of his golden boots, he

leapt high, gripped the plinth at
the top of the column, and pulled
himself up.

Below, Tom saw Silexa draw back
a massive paw. *BOOF!* She smashed
it into the bottom of the pillar. The

sudden jolt almost threw Tom from his feet, but he kicked off the falling column and leapt for the next in the row, landing squarely on top. In one bound, Silexa reached the base, roared with anger and struck out

once more, smashing the stone with
her paw. Tom jumped to the next high
plinth and the next, but the Beast
kept pace with him easily, felling the
colonnade like a row of dominoes, the
air filling with rubble and dust.

Tom reached the last column and, with nowhere to go, braced himself and leapt for the ground. A mighty *CRASH!* rang out behind him as he landed, spinning round and seeing that Silexa had smashed down the final pillar in the row. The huge plinth from the top plummeted towards the cat's head. But before it struck her, the Beast dissolved into a billowing cloud of smoke, and vanished.

Elenna reached Tom's side, breathing heavily, her hair and face streaked with dust.

"What now?" she said, wiping the sweat from her brow. "How can we defeat a Beast that can turn herself into a shadow?"

Tom frowned, her words triggering an idea… "My white jewel!" he said. "Maybe to fight her, I need to be a shadow too!"

Elenna's brows knitted together. "But if you use your white jewel to become a shadow, you'll have to leave your body behind. You'd be helpless — Silexa could kill you with one paw-strike."

Tom nodded. "So we'd better not let her find me. We'll need to create a diversion…"

Elenna smiled grimly. "Bait. Leave that to me."

They slipped behind a low wall and into the least damaged building left – it had no ceiling, but was better than nothing. Tom crouched in a corner, took a deep breath, and put a hand to the white jewel in his belt. A strange, cold feeling ran over his skin, his vision blurring, then refocussing. Everything looked the same, but he felt light and empty. When he tried to draw a breath, nothing came. *A shadow doesn't need air.* Tom stood and stepped away from his lifeless body. Elenna met his gaze and nodded. Then she sprinted off, quickly taking up position on the mound of rubble that had once been Silexa's temple. Tom stole one last look at his empty body, suppressed a shudder, then set

off, darting behind a pillar to wait.

Soon, he heard the soft crunch of
paws on rubble, and peered out to
see Silexa stalking towards Elenna.
The huge cat's tail lashed from side
to side as she moved.

"I'm glad you came!" Elenna called to the Beast, fitting an arrow to her bow. "Now for some target practice!" But instead of creeping closer, Silexa

lifted her great head, nostrils flaring as she scented the air. Then she turned slowly, still sniffing, her ears pricked and her whiskers twitching.

"I'm over here!" Elenna shouted. Silexa ignored her and padded on – straight towards the building where Tom's helpless body lay.

*The Beast can smell me!* Tom realised, terror fizzing through him. He measured the distance with his eyes, but he knew he'd never reach his body in time. Silexa picked her way easily over the low wall that sheltered Tom's defenceless form. After letting out a victorious roar, she lowered her head and opened her massive jaws. Gripped with panic,

Tom wondered what would happen when Silexa devoured his body. Would he be trapped as a shadow, for ever?

*Or will I simply disappear...?*

# BATTLE OF THE SHADOWS

Staring with horror at the giant Beast about to devour his body, and unable to save himself, Tom waited for the end.

"I said, I'm over here, you dim-witted kitten!" Elenna cried, a frenzied note of panic in her voice. Almost lazily, Silexa turned her

head to glance in Elenna's direction.
At the same instant, Elenna fired
her arrow. *Thwack!* It sank deep
into one of Silexa's red eyes. The
giant cat shook her head, snarling
in agony. Her body began to fade,

becoming shadowy and fraying at the edges, spiralling into tendrils of mist. But Tom was already racing towards the Beast, running with shadow-speed as swift and as silent as the wind. He reached Silexa just as her smoky form began to fade, but with his eyes fixed on the point where her broad chest had been, Tom knew his mark. He vaulted over the low wall, drew back his shadow sword and thrust it upwards into the Beast's smoky pelt, burying it to the hilt, deep in her shadow heart.

As Tom drew his sword from her chest, Silexa shook her head from side to side. Her huge form

flickered, briefly becoming flesh and fur before returning to shadow once more. Tom dived towards his own body, feeling a rush of warmth and relief as he became living flesh and blood. He let out a shuddering breath, then gathered himself, and stood up.

Silexa was staggering away through the remains of the colonnade, her body swaying from side to side, and her form switching between solid flesh and swirling smoke. She dragged herself on, leaving behind a trail of dark blood, before clambering on to the ruins of the temple. With a mighty shudder, Silexa sank down on the rubble and fell still. Familiar cries of anguish filled Tom's ears as the cat-people reappeared from their hiding places, staring at the fallen Beast whom they worshipped.

Tom and Elenna hurried to Silexa's side, where they were quickly joined by Aleesa. With a jolt of fear, Tom noticed that the Beast's broad chest was still rising and falling. One huge eye remained open, a narrow slit of fiery red. Tom lifted his sword, but, as he watched, the glowing red of the eye changed to a brilliant emerald green. Silexa curled her vast body around itself, tucking her tail and paws into the comfortable pose of a sleeping cat.

Tom reached for the red jewel in

his belt and heard the Beast's voice as it should have sounded – a soft, velvety purr. *Thank you, Master of the Beasts*, she said. *Now I am free...* Her green eye closed, and with a crackling sound, her body hardened to black, shiny rock. Another sound started up. The clatter of falling bricks. Tom turned in alarm, but his fear quickly changed to awe as he saw the bricks weren't falling. They were rising!

"It's a miracle!" Aleesa cried, her voice filled with wonder. Chunks of masonry clattered across the ground, rolling together to form pillars and buildings once more. The rubble beneath Tom's feet trembled.

He, Elenna and Aleesa quickly leapt away as the temple they had been standing on re-formed itself around the statue of the giant cat. Tom gazed in amazement at the magnificent buildings all around him. And the colour! Where most of the ruins had been plain brown sandstone, now bright splashes of ruby, emerald and sapphire coloured the walls. Vines, heavy with flowers, coiled around the pillars of the colonnade, and the once silent fountains bubbled and sang, sending out glittering cascades of water.

"Silexa has restored our city!" Aleesa said, her eyes shining with tears of joy. Ezra bounded to his mother's side, and she threw her arms around him. He mewed a few hopeful-sounding words, pointing towards the temple. Aleesa nodded, resting her cheek against her son's sandy hair.

"Yes, she is safe. And our home is as it should be," she said, smiling. Then she turned to Tom and Elenna. "I am sorry that I distrusted you. You have fulfilled your promise to help us, a thousand times over!" Suddenly, her smile faded. "But we have an apology to make. Although we pursued the wizard, Zargon, we were unable to capture him."

Tom sighed. "I am not surprised he's made himself scarce. He still has one more weapon at his disposal. He will already be looking for the next Beast to awaken. I am afraid we must go at once."

"Yes, but which way should we go?" Elenna asked.

"There, I think I can help you,"
Aleesa said. She pointed far into the
distance, where a great mountain
rose up stark and grey against the
blue of the sky. Tom saw what at
first he took to be a long, white
cloud at the summit. But as he
watched it billow and flow, he
realised it was smoke, pouring from
a crater.

"That volcano has been dormant
for centuries," Aleesa said. "Legend
tells of a mighty Beast buried at its
heart." Tom and Elenna turned to
each other and exchanged weary
but determined nods.

"Then that is where we must
go," Tom said. "Although it would

take magic to reach the summit before Zargon does."

Elenna put her hand firmly on Tom's shoulder. "We don't need magic to defeat the wizard," she said. "We've already proved three times that we've got something far more powerful."

Tom tipped his head, puzzled.

Elenna smiled. "Courage!"

## THE END

# CONGRATULATIONS, YOU HAVE COMPLETED THIS QUEST!

At the end of each chapter you were awarded a special gold coin. The QUEST in this book was worth an amazing 8 coins.

Look at the Beast Quest totem picture opposite to see how far you've come in your journey to become

MASTER OF THE BEASTS.

The more books you read, the more coins you will collect!

Do you want your own Beast Quest Totem?

1. Cut out and collect the coin below
2. Go to the Beast Quest website
3. Download and print out your totem
4. Add your coin to the totem

www.beastquest.co.uk

READ THE BOOKS, COLLECT THE COINS!
EARN COINS FOR EVERY CHAPTER YOU READ!

550+ COINS
MASTER OF
THE BEASTS

410 COINS
HERO

350 COINS
WARRIOR

230 COINS
KNIGHT

180 COINS
SQUIRE

44 COINS
PAGE

8 COINS
APPRENTICE

# READ ALL THE BOOKS IN SERIES 26:
## THE FOUR MASTERS!

**TEKNOS**
**THE OCEAN CRAWLER**

**MALLIX**
**THE SILENT STALKER**

**SILEXA**
**THE STONE CAT**

**KYRON**
**LORD OF FIRE**

*Don't miss the next exciting Beast Quest book: KYRON, LORD OF FIRE!*

*Read on for a sneak peek...*

# THE STRIDING GATE

Tom's legs ached and his head swam from clambering over endless rocks under the baking sun. Having left the city of Viga behind them, he and Elenna were now picking their way through the crumbled ruins of an

even older settlement. Tom stopped
to push the sweaty hair back from
his face, then lifted his eyes to the
smoking volcano in the distance,

suppressing a growl of frustration.

*It doesn't seem any closer at all!*

Elenna came to a halt beside him and leant on her knees, breathing heavily. She and Tom had fought three mighty Beasts in as many days, leaving them both close to exhaustion. Each Beast had been unleashed on Tangala by the Evil Wizard, Zargon, using magical weapons he had stolen from the crypt beneath Queen Aroha's palace in Pania.

Tom and Elenna's most recent battle had been against a giant stone cat called Silexa. They had managed to free Silexa from Zargon's curse, saving the cat-folk of Viga in the process. But always one step ahead, Zargon had escaped and was now planning to awaken a fourth and final Beast from beneath the volcano. According to the cat-folk, the volcano had lain dormant for hundreds of years, but even from here, Tom could feel its distant rumble though the ground — deep and ominous, like thunder on a summer's night. *While there's blood in my veins, Zargon will never win!* he vowed.

"How far do you think we still have to go?" Elenna asked, shading her eyes as she gazed towards the volcano.

Tom forced his tired shoulders

back and stood straight. "Further than I'd like," he said. "We had better hurry." He took a slug of water from his bottle, but it was gritty and warm, barely touching his thirst.

"There's more smoke than before," Elenna said, frowning at the yellow clouds that wreathed the volcano's summit. "That can't be a good sign."

"It is not," a gruff female voice said from behind them. Tom and Elenna turned to see a tall and powerfully built warrior woman. She was dressed in full armour except for her helmet, which she held under one arm. Her short, spiked hair was pale blonde, and her sun-browned face looked weary, but her sombre eyes

were keen and sharp. Tom tensed,
ready to defend against any attack,
until he realised he could still see the
heat haze of the desert through her

form. *A ghost!*

Tom had already met two such spirits, who had each helped him and Elenna reach the next stage of their Quest.

"You must be one of the four brave candidates who perished defeating the ancient Beasts of Tangala," Tom said, dipping his head respectfully.

The woman nodded. "I am Ofelia," she told them. "I fell in battle with Silexa. You have done well to survive the Beast's wrath. But the forces that disturbed her rest are not yet vanquished — Evil stirs beneath the mountain. I fear that before this day is done, there will be fire and devastation."

Dread tightened about Tom's chest like a vice. "Then Zargon must already have reached the volcano," he said. "We are too late!"

The ancient warrior's lips became a thin, grim line. "You are late, yes, but there is still a chance you can stop this Evil. Follow me." She turned on her heel and strode away. Tom and Elenna exchanged a wary glance, then followed as Ofelia led them towards a pile of jumbled grey rocks.

"This was once a magical portal," the ghost said, gesturing at the rubble. "Though it was destroyed long ago, some of its power yet remains."

Tom noticed that many of the

rocks had worn, straight edges, while a few were curved. But all were badly weathered and cracked.

Elenna frowned. "As portals go, this one doesn't look too promising. Surely we'd need to go through it?"

"Indeed," Ofelia said. "As it lies, the Striding Gate can take you nowhere. But that doesn't mean it can't be rebuilt." Looking carefully, Tom could see the faint imprint of zigzag lines etched along the length of each brick.

"There's a pattern we can use as a guide," he said. "But without any kind of mortar, it won't be easy."

The woman raised an eyebrow. "Who said anything about 'easy'?"

she asked.

Tom and Elenna got to work, sorting the stones into order and setting them flat on the ground, until they had made the shape of a doorway. It looked slightly taller than they were, and wide enough for them to pass through side by side.

Working as fast as they could in the stifling heat, they built the sides upwards, balancing the worn blocks on top of each other. Each new brick made Tom's stacks wobble, threatening to topple them. Sweat made Tom's hands slippery, but soon he and Elenna had two rickety-looking pillars. Three blocks remained: two huge curved sections, and the keystone.

Tom stood back, shaking the ache from his arms. "Now for the tricky part."

Together they built the arched section on the ground, slotting the keystone in last of all.

"I'll hold the sides steady while you hoist it into place," said Elenna. Tom nodded, then lifted the final assembled pieces with trembling arms. Even with the strength of the golden breastplate, it was tough work. He extended his arms, and slotted the arched section on top of the vertical stacks. For a moment, the whole doorway wobbled, but it held.

Ofelia gave a satisfied nod. "Well

done," she said.

"How does the Striding Gate
work?" Tom asked her, eyeing the
precarious structure.

"Clear your mind of all other thoughts, and focus on where you want to be as you step through," she said. "But I must warn you, even before the portal fell, it was perilous. If you allow your mind to stray, even for an instant, the magic will fail. In the past, it was even known for people to disappear into the gate, never to be seen again. Who knows where they ended up?"

Read
*KYRON, LORD OF FIRE*
to find out what happens next!

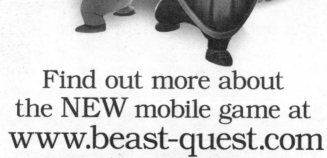

Find out more about
the NEW mobile game at
www.beast-quest.com